W9-AKY-097

School Corporation
Mishawaka, Indiana

MARY FRANK SCHOOL LIBRARY

T 7857

E
Mog

Mogensen, Jan

Lost and Found Teddy

Lost and Found
Teddy

For a free color catalog describing Gareth Stevens' list of high-quality children's books, call 1-800-341-3569 (USA) or 1-800-461-9120 (Canada).

TEDDY TALES

Teddy in the Undersea Kingdom
Teddy's Christmas Gift
When Teddy Woke Early
Teddy and the Chinese Dragon
Teddy Runs Away
Teddy's Birthday Bugle
Lost and Found Teddy

Library of Congress Cataloging-in-Publication Data

Mogensen, Jan.
    [Bamses ven. English]
    Lost and found Teddy / Jan Mogensen.
        p.   cm.
    Translation of: Bamses ven.
    Summary: Separated from their children during a train trip, Teddy and Noodle wait anxiously in the train station's lost and found office.
    ISBN 0-8368-0432-5
    [1. Lost and found possessions--Fiction. 2. Teddy bears--Fiction. 3. Railroads--Trains--Fiction.] I. Title.
PZ7.M7274Lo   1990
[E]--dc20
                                      90-10077

North American edition first published in 1990 by
Gareth Stevens Children's Books
1555 North RiverCenter Drive, Suite 201
Milwaukee, Wisconsin 53212, USA

U.S. edition copyright © 1990. Text copyright © 1990 by Gareth Stevens, Inc. First published as *Bamses ven* in Denmark by Borgens Forlag with an original text copyright © 1983 by Jan Mogensen. Illustrations copyright © 1983 by Jan Mogensen.

All rights reserved. No part of this book may be reproduced or used in any form or by any means without permission in writing from Gareth Stevens, Inc.

English text: MaryLee Knowlton

Printed in the United States of America

1 2 3 4 5 6 7 8 9 96 95 94 93 92 91 90

Lost and Found
Teddy

Jan Mogensen

Gareth Stevens Children's Books
MILWAUKEE

Max and Norah were taking the train to their grandmother's house. They were traveling alone for the first time.

Laughing excitedly, the children were busy planning the fun they would have. They were not paying much attention to the station stops. Teddy was worried. Would they get off at the right place?

The train slowed to a standstill. Suddenly, Max realized where they were. "This is our stop," he yelled. "Let's go!" He and Norah grabbed their bags and dashed out of the train.

But they didn't grab Teddy.

Teddy tried to call out to them, but the train gave a long blast of its whistle and started moving. No one heard him. He'd been forgotten.

As the train picked up speed, Teddy could hardly keep from crying. "How could they forget me?" he wondered sadly. The train clacked and rattled along through the countryside, carrying Teddy farther and farther away from Max and Norah.

Then it began to slow down again as it neared the next station.

The brakes squealed as the train came to a stop. Teddy climbed onto the armrest to look out the window.

Out on the platform, Teddy saw two children with their mother. They looked nice enough, but Teddy was afraid anyway.

"What if they are teddy bear thieves?" he thought in a panic. "I must hide!"

The children boarded the train and sat down in the seat right behind Teddy. They chattered happily about their trip and didn't notice him.

"They seem friendly," thought Teddy, "but I'm not taking any chances." He tucked himself behind the window curtain.

The train started rolling again. Teddy hardly breathed for fear of being discovered.

After what seemed like a very, very long time, the train came to another stop. The children and their mother got off, but Teddy stayed hidden, waiting for the train to move again. "It will come to the end of the line and go back to where we started," he thought. "Max and Norah will surely be waiting for me."

But the train did not move.

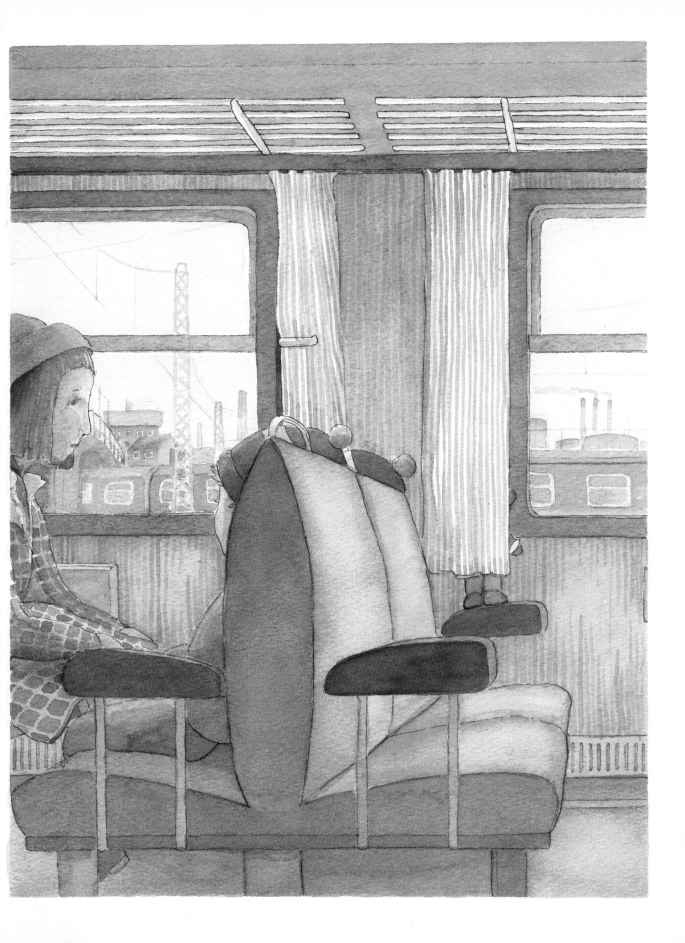

Someone was in the train car. Teddy could hear footsteps. He peeked around the edge of the curtain.

A train conductor was coming down the aisle. He was looking under all the seats. "Those silly kids," the man chuckled. "They always forget something."

Just then he saw Teddy's feet sticking out from beneath the curtain. "And here's what they forgot today!" he laughed.

He grabbed poor Teddy, tucked him tightly under his arm, and left the train.

When they reached the depot, the conductor plopped Teddy down on the ticket counter. Already sitting there was a strange-looking little fellow. Teddy thought he looked like a mixture of pig, kangaroo, a small dog, and a lot of worry. The creature looked more worried than even Teddy felt.

"You two stay here and get acquainted while I make my last round," said the conductor. Then he was gone.

"How do you do?" said Teddy, politely. "I'm Teddy."

"I'm Noodle Noggin," said the little fellow. "Are you lost, too?"

"Well, either I'm lost or Max and Norah are lost. It all comes out the same, doesn't it, Mr. Noodle Noggin?" replied Teddy sadly.

"Yes, I guess so," agreed Noodle. "By the way, you can call me 'Noodle.' "

"There. We're closed for the night," said the conductor, poking his head into the room. He reached in and snapped out all the lights, except for a green bulb under the clock.

"At least we have a night-light," said Noodle, but he didn't sound happy about it.

Teddy and Noodle sat without speaking for a long time. Teddy thought about Norah and how tightly she always hugged him. Then he thought about Max's bright smile and snappy eyes. "Oh, I feel so sorry for myself," Teddy thought, and he felt tears coming to his eyes.

"I've never slept alone before," Noodle whispered in a scared, shivery voice. "I want to go home to Ellie."

"But you're not alone. Teddy is here," said Teddy, wiping his eyes quickly. He put his arm around the trembling Noodle.

But Noodle couldn't be comforted. "Ellie, Ellie, Ellie," he sobbed.

"Put your little head down in my lap," whispered Teddy, and he covered Noodle with his coat. As Noodle cried softly, Teddy rubbed his back, and soon the two sad friends were asleep.

When morning came, the conductor returned, carrying a big box. He wrote LOST AND FOUND on the side, and in went Noodle and Teddy.

All day, Teddy and Noodle lay in the box. To pass the time, they told each other stories.

"Once Max built me a boat," Teddy told his new friend. "But it leaked, and I nearly drowned in the bathtub. Norah hung me outside by my ears for the rest of the day until I dried out!" he laughed.

"Sometimes Ellie says 'Naughty Noodle' and then she pretends to spank me," laughed Noodle. "Then she says she's so, so sorry, and she hugs and kisses me."

They talked about playing dress-up with their children. "I have a king's outfit," Teddy boasted. "I have a raincoat and umbrella," bragged Noodle.

Suddenly the friends felt themselves moving. Someone was carrying their box!

Teddy and Noodle arrived at their next stop — the Lost and Found Office. Unfamiliar hands took them out of their box and carried them down a long hall lined with shelves. Oof! They were shoved into an empty space on a crowded shelf.

Teddy and Noodle found themselves surrounded by bags and boxes and suitcases and umbrellas — all sorts of things that people had forgotten on the train. On the same shelf sprawled a forlorn-looking dog with floppy ears.

In a voice sad and low, he said, "Hello, friends. You do know that you've come to a dreadful place, don't you?"

"A dreadful place?" echoed Noodle. His voice was shivery again, and he trembled as he clung to Teddy's arm.

"Dreadful!" exclaimed Teddy. "This is the Lost and Found. This is where they'll come to look for us. This is a good place to be!"

24

"But people only come here looking for their watches and glasses," said the dog. "After a month, if you're still here, someone can buy you and take you home. I'm going up for sale in two days. I hope someone buys me and takes me away from here."

Now Teddy, too, was trembling with fear, but he tried to look brave for Noodle. Neither of them wanted to be sold to a new home.

"I'm so frightened," Noodle whispered. "So frightened."

"Frightened? I'll show you something that will frighten you!" said a fierce voice. Thump! A tough-looking ape dropped down from the top shelf, knotting up his face to look mean. He waved his big fists in front of Noodle.

"You're a weird-looking thing," the ape sneered at poor Noodle, who was cowering as far back on the shelf as he could get. "Repeat after me, 'I am weird.'"

Noodle was so frightened, he couldn't say anything at all.

"'I am weird,'" growled the ape again. "Say it."

"That's enough of that mean talk," said Teddy sternly. "You stop your bad behavior."

"Bad behavior? Bad behavior!" roared the ape. "I'll show you bad behavior."

Just as his long arms reached out to grab Teddy, everyone heard voices in the outer office.

"We have come to get Teddy," said a girl's voice.

"We left him on the train yesterday," a boy's voice added.

"It's Max and Norah," Teddy cried with relief.

The ape jumped back up to the top shelf as the door opened. Two hands picked up Teddy and carried him out. He looked back at Noodle, now frozen with fear as he saw Teddy leaving.

"Oh, Teddy! Sweet old Teddy," cried Norah and Max as they hugged and kissed him. "We thought you were gone forever."

Teddy tried to feel happy, but he couldn't forget Noodle's scared little face. What would happen to him now? Who would save him from that awful ape?

Suddenly, the outer door opened and a sobbing little girl came in with her mother.

"I don't know quite how to explain this," the mother said, "but my daughter lost her stuffed animal on the train. It's gray and looks something like a kangaroo, something like a pig, and a little like a dog."

"His name is Noodle," said the little girl. "Is he here?"

Teddy had never felt such joy. It was Ellie. Noodle was saved! As they left the Lost and Found, Teddy caught one last glimpse of his friend happily riding in Ellie's backpack.

"That's a sweet-looking little guy, isn't he, Teddy?" said Max. "Anyone you know?"